Ela Are
275 Moh
P9-DHL-912
(847) 438-3433
www.eapl.org
31241008099148
JUN 2014

Toe Shoe Mouse

by **JAN CARR**

illustrated by **JENNIFER A. BELL**

Holiday House / New York

For Phoebe and Esme, my little dancers—J. C.

For V and S—J. B.

Printed and Bound in November 2013 at Tien Wah Press, Johor Bahru, Johor, Malaysia.
The artwork was rendered in pencil and colored digitally.
www.holidayhouse.com
First Edition
1 3 5 7 9 10 8 6 4 2

Library of Congress Cataloging-in-Publication Data
Carr, Jan.
Toe shoe mouse / by Jan Carr ; illustrated by Jennifer A. Bell. — 1st ed.
p. cm.
Summary: Chased into a theater by a cat, a mouse becomes entranced
by the ballet dancers on stage and comes to be friends
with one of them.
ISBN 978-0-8234-2406-1 (hardcover)
[1. Ballet dancing—Fiction. 2. Mice—Fiction.]
I. Bell, Jennifer (Jennifer A.), 1977- ill. II. Title.
PZ7.C22947Toe 2014
[E]—dc23
2011046693

I will not go into the disturbing details of how I arrived at the ballet. I will say only that it involved a cat with glittering teeth and cruel claws, and a chase through the sewers of the city. I escaped through a hole that was much too small for a cat.

And that is how I found myself inside a very old and very grand theater.

I climbed up to a plush velvet seat and spied a stage where people were moving to music. The music made me want to move too. So there on my velvet stage, I did my own little mouse dance. And I realized, *I'd like to stay here!*

Suddenly the music stopped.

"Take your places!" called a voice.

Good idea, I thought. I set to work.

I gnawed a cozy nest for myself in the soft velvet of the seat. But I had barely settled in when I was startled by the arrival of a gentleman who thought the seat was his.

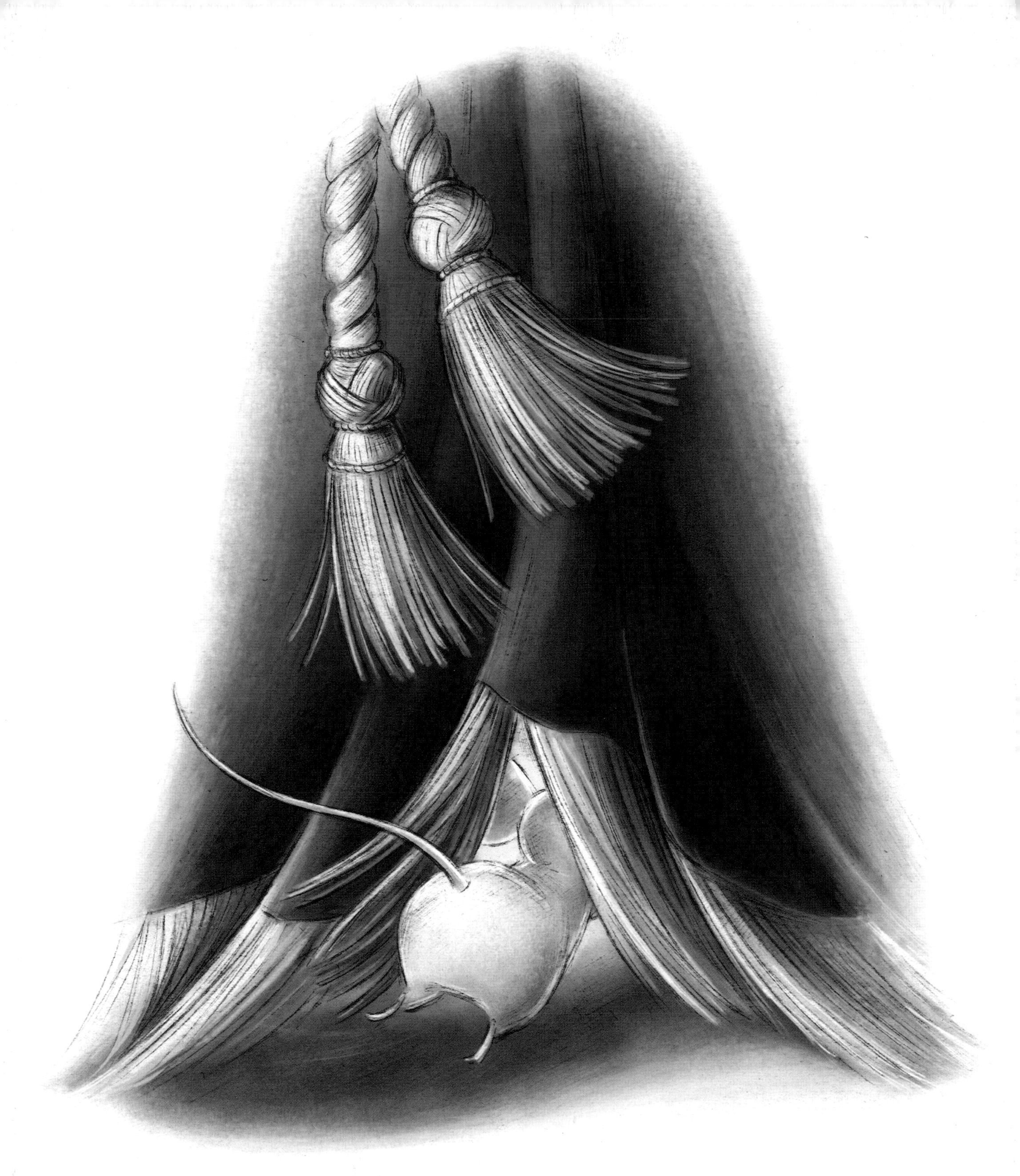

I dashed toward the stage. Immediately, a mob of people began chasing me.

Eek! They had
big, heavy boots
and—oh no!—sharp,
flashing swords!

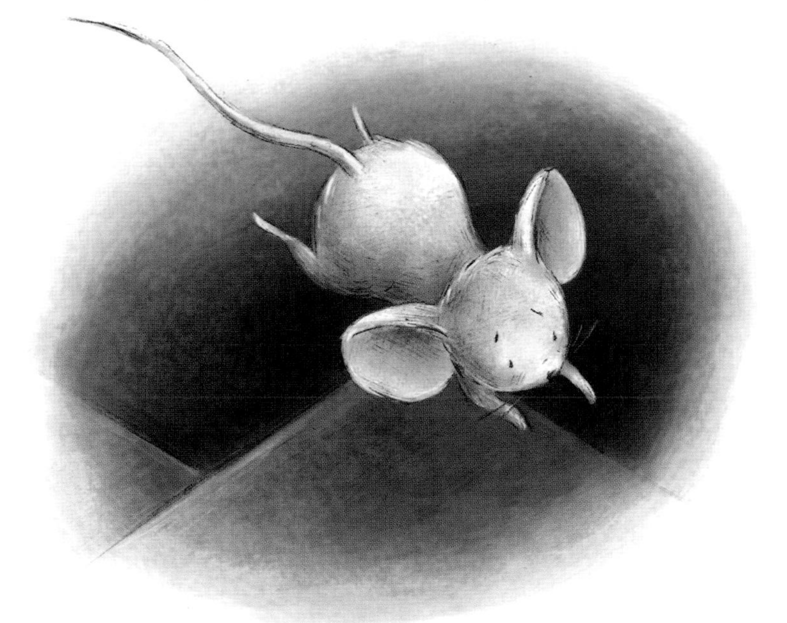

I ran. Up steps, under doors, until I found myself in a safe, quiet room.

Tucked in a corner was a small, satin crevice. It was just the right size for hiding and was padded with a soft bed of lamb's wool.

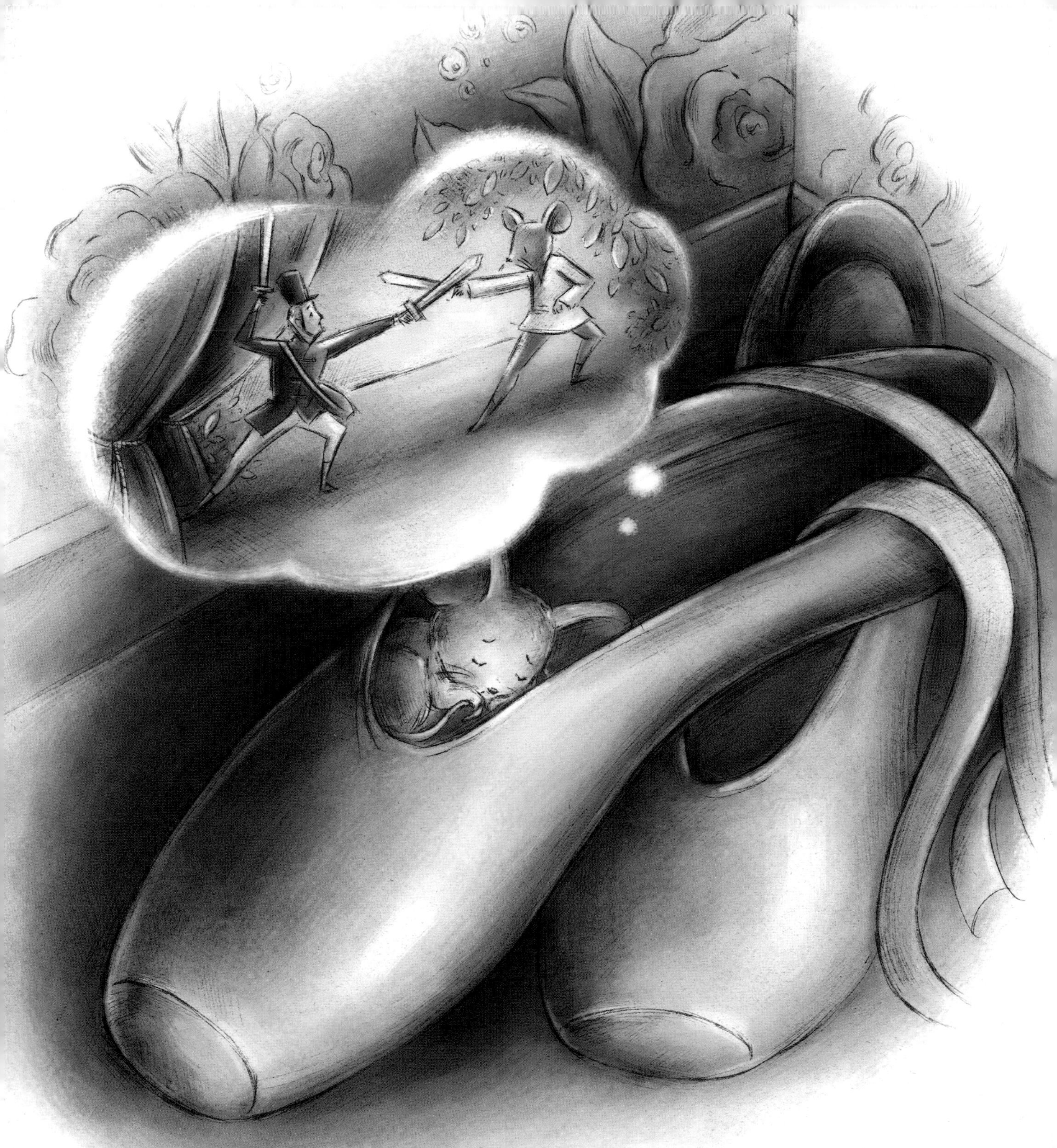

Calmed by the animal scent of the wool, I fell into
a fitful sleep, dreaming of sword fights and soldiers.

When I awoke, someone was in the room: a young woman I recognized from the stage. She stretched one leg high above her. How did she do that?

"Céleste!" someone called.
Even her name was graceful!

The young woman left, and I slipped out after her to look for food.

I was happy to find a few tasty tidbits and decided to bring some back for Céleste.

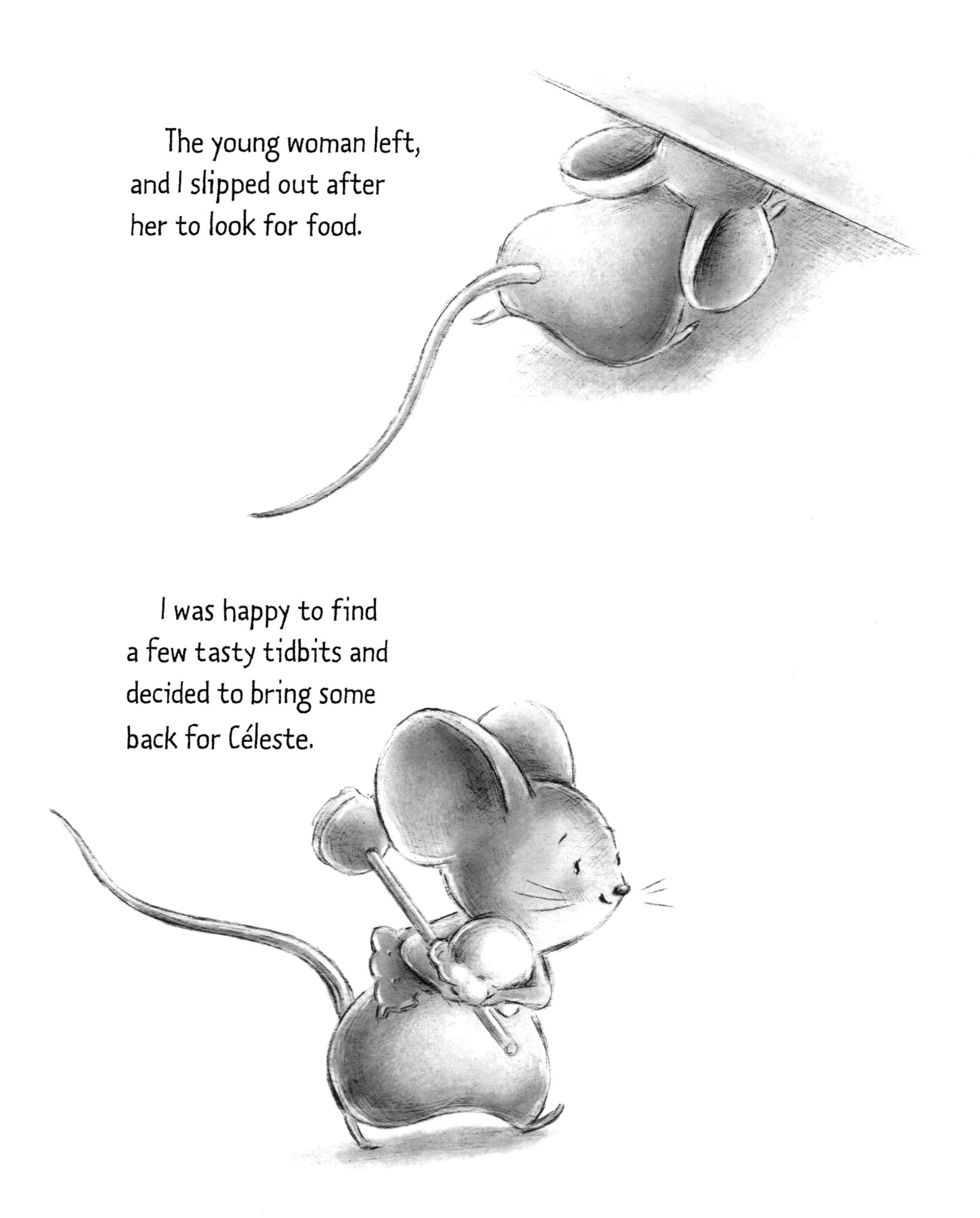

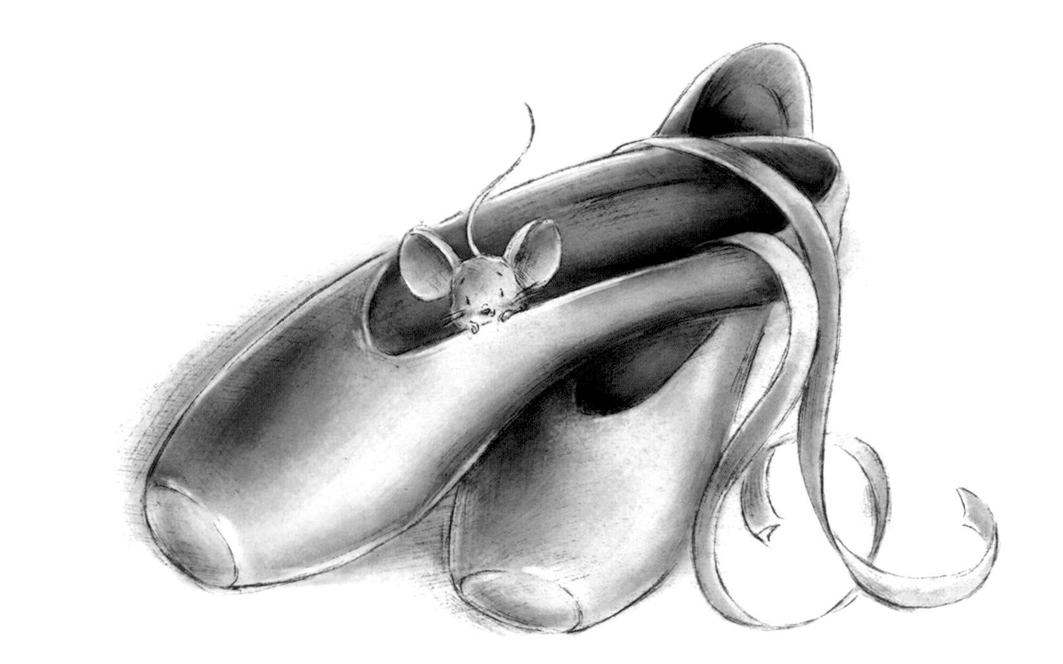

Because I was curious to see if she'd like them, I hid again in the snug satin pocket. But in the morning, Céleste didn't eat a thing. Maybe she didn't like my choices?

That night I collected even tastier bits. But Céleste looked more puzzled than pleased.

The next time I set out, I came nose-to-toe with the custodian.

To escape the slam of his broom, I slipped under a door.

There I discovered spools of rickrack and braid. I snipped a strand with my teeth, brought it back, and arranged it artfully for Céleste.

When she discovered it, Céleste swung a leg back and forth, loose limbed and happy.

The next night I brought her a curl of ribbon. And the night after that a circlet of sequins.

I could tell that she liked them. Her long legs scissored and stretched.

But suddenly
Céleste swooped over,
her nose grazing mine.

My instincts shouted *Run!*, so I tore out the door.

As I skittered down the steps, the custodian spotted me. He chased me to the tiny hole in the basement, and I squeezed through—just in time!—leaving the theater behind.

I will not dwell on what happened in the dank underground passages. I will say only that it involved a pack of ruthless rats. I hid from them, my heart pounding, and thought longingly of the ballet. I hummed a snippet of music I remembered, and my tail began to sway.

Oh no! The rats spotted it! They chased me down gullies, up gutters, and back through the hole that was too small even for a rat.

Exhausted, I headed for my pink satin bed. But it wasn't there! In its place was a cookie shaped like a mouse. I nibbled at its crumbly sweetness. Had Céleste left it for me?

When I looked up, there was Céleste, crouched down and staring at me. Would she screech? Take a broom to me? Chase me away forever?

"Thank you for the presents," she said. "Why did you run away?"

Céleste gave me a name, Tendu, but you can call me Stretch. She also tied a sash around me so everyone would know I'm her pet.

Now, every day, I listen to music with my fantastic,
elastic friend. And—with my new friend, in my new home—

I dance.